YOU ARE ABOUT TO READ

LIKE, MAD

. . . especially if you haven't paid for this book, **and** you want to finish it before the man spots you!

SO HERE ARE A FEW THINGS YOU SHOULD KNOW . . . in case you want to change your mind!

LIKE, MAD
    . . . IS NOT "SQUARE!"
It's much longer than it is wide!

LIKE, MAD
    . . . IS REAL "COOL!"
If you keep it in the refrigerator!

LIKE, MAD
    . . . IS "THE MOST!"
The most asinine stuff you've read!

LIKE, MAD
    . . . IS "THE END!"

The end of a long line of successful paperback books if it doesn't sell . . .

LIKE, MAD

Other MAD Books You'll Enjoy

This publication, an exact reprint of Like, MAD *(1960), faithfully reproduces the advertisement above contained in the original. Readers are cautioned against relying on this advertising and should not consider any of it, or offers with it, valid in any way.*

WILLIAM M. GAINES'S

LIKE,

Albert B. Feldstein, Editor

new york
www.ibooksinc.com

DISTRIBUTED BY SIMON & SCHUSTER, INC

Front cover painting by Kelly Freas

Special thanks to:
Grant Geissman;
Nick Meglin (*MAD* Magazine);

An ibooks, inc. Book

Distributed by Simon & Schuster, Inc.
1230 Avenue of the Americas, New York, NY 10020

ibooks, inc.
24 West 25th Street
New York, NY 10010

The ibooks World Wide Web Site Address is:
http://www.ibooksinc.com

Visit www.madmag.com

ISBN 0-7434-7977-7
First ibooks, inc. printing January 2004
10 9 8 7 6 5 4 3 2 1

Printed in the U.S.A.

CONTENTS

INTRODUCTION
by Grant Geissman

Like, MAD is the ninth book in the series of anniversary reprints—published by ibooks—of the early *MAD* paperbacks.

The original edition of *Like, MAD*—the fourth *MAD* paperback to be issued under the Signet Books imprint—appeared in September 1960. The title and cover image to *Like, MAD* is *MAD*'s spin on the beatnik/bohemian types that were then populating New York's Greenwich Village. The book's title also plays on beatnik lingo ("It's like, mad, baby!"), and has a very different pronunciation than the more current "Valley Girl" usage of the word (as in "Like, you know?"). The book's cover was rendered by revered illustrator Kelly Freas (the magazine's featured cover artist at the time), and is considered to be one of the artist's all-time classic *MAD* covers—paperback or otherwise.

Unlike the previous *MAD* paperbacks, all of the material appearing here (with one minor exception) dates from after *MAD* creator Harvey Kurtzman's departure from the magazine. Longtime E.C. artist/writer/editor Al Feldstein took over as *MAD*'s editor with issue #29 (September-October 1956); almost all of the material in this book is collected from issues that appeared from that point onward. (See the Introduction to the ibooks edition of *Utterly MAD* for an in-depth discussion of Kurtzman's abrupt departure from the magazine and the reasons behind it.) Articles attributed here as written by the "staff" were put together collectively by the triumvirate of *MAD* staffers Al Feldstein, Jerry DeFuccio, and Nick Meglin.

Opening this collection is "Foreign Movies" (*MAD* #33, May-June 1957, illustrated by Wallace Wood and written by the staff), a look at how the subtitles in foreign movies might not always match up to the action on the screen. Wood here uses a variety of techniques to approximate the grain and texture of black and white film.

"The Top Bomb Song Hits" (*MAD* #36, November-December 1957, written by the staff) was originally a one-pager, that, apart from the magazine cover illustration, is among the relatively few *MAD* pieces that consist nearly entirely of text. Interestingly, the magazine cover illustration in this piece was by Al Feldstein (note the small "AF" signature), one of the very few pieces of art Feldstein did for *MAD*. Another short text piece, "The Railroad Timetable," is from *MAD* #33, May-June 1957. A hybrid of text and minimal illustration (also from issue #33, written by the staff) can be found in "Dead Letters."

"*MAD* Coats of Arms" (*MAD* #34, July-August

1957, written by Frank Jacobs) is one of a number of interior pieces done for the magazine by Kelly Freas before he took over the duties as *MAD*'s regular cover artist from Norman Mingo.

The two "Scenes We'd Like to See" features (from *MAD* #27, April 1956 and *MAD* #29, September-October 1956) were both written and illustrated by Phil Interlandi. Interlandi did about nine of these "Scenes We'd Like to See" pages for the early magazine version of *MAD*, and then went on to a successful career as a *Playboy* cartoonist. After Interlandi's departure, the feature was illustrated by Joe Orlando, who had previously done work for many of the E.C. comics, including *PANIC*, the Feldstein-edited sister publication of the *MAD* comic book. Orlando's work is represented in this collection by "*MAD* Eating Utensils" (*MAD* #35, September-October 1957, written by the staff). Amazingly, quite a few of the wacky products depicted here might actually work, and could even be in demand if they were to be introduced to the marketplace!

"*MAD*'s Picture Phone Backdrops" (*MAD* #34, July-August 1957, written by the staff) was illustrated by George Woodbridge, a friend of staffer Nick Meglin's from the School of Visual Arts. Woodbridge originally had his sights set on a career in book and magazine illustration, but through Meglin he was introduced to many of the E.C. and *MAD* gang, including Harvey Kurtzman, Al Feldstein, Bill Gaines, Al Williamson, Frank Frazetta, Jerry DeFuccio and *MAD* art director John Putnam. He soon came to appreciate the artistic freedom the magazine represented (while also offering

an outlet for his humorous side), and Woodbridge quickly became a regular. Apart from his work with *MAD*, Woodbridge is considered to be a expert in the field of military and historical uniforms, and he has illustrated a number of books on the subject, including *American Military Dress and Equipage.*

An unlicensed early 1960s post-card copying the "Like, MAD" cover, released by IMPKO.

"Motorist Beware!" (from *MAD* #30, November-December 1956, written by Herb Goldstein) is the very first article done for the magazine by Bob Clarke. Clarke segued into *MAD* after working for various Madison Avenue ad agencies, and—like George Woodbridge—he had grown tired of the restrictions of the job. Clarke instantly became a *MAD* regular and, nearly fifty years later, he still does occasional pieces for the magazine. Clarke's work is very well-represented in this volume. "The *MAD* Dating Technique" (*MAD* #32, March-April 1957, written by the staff) is considered to be an early classic, as is "Camera Comparison" (from *MAD* #31, January-February 1957, written by Arnie Rosen). "Raw Guts" parodies a genre in magazine publishing that doesn't exist anymore in this post-feminist age: the "sex, bondage, blood, and guts" men's magazines of the 1950s and 1960s. "Raw Guts" focuses more on the "blood and guts" side of the genre, but there were plenty of these magazines whose covers featured paintings of provocatively-posed women (usually tied up) that needed to be saved from some menacing force by a "real man."

IMPKO also had a line of decals, for car windshields and bikes. This full-color unauthorized early 1960s decal also borrows from "Like, MAD."

Wallace Wood does another on-target job of comic strip mimicry in "Nansy" (from *MAD* #32, March-April 1957), which presents the *Nancy* strip as other artists

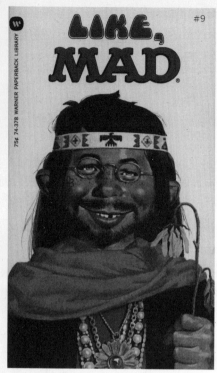

75¢ 74-378 WARNER PAPERBACK LIBRARY

#9

The "beatnik" image was replaced by a "hippie" visage with Norman Mingo's cover for the November, 1973 reissue.

might do her. Created by Ernie Bushmiller, *The World Encyclopedia of Comics* states that "Nancy was perhaps the most widely-followed strip character of the 1950s and early 1960s." Nancy originally appeared as early as the 1920s as the niece of the eponymously-named *Fritzi Ritz*, but by 1940 Bushmiller changed the strip to *Nancy* and moved the simply-drawn character to center stage. As popular as the strip was, it was considered by many to be infuriatingly simple (even simple-minded) both in concept and execution.

Wood's art nicely frames "The Potrzebie System of Weights and Measures" (*MAD* #33, May-June 1957, written by Donald Knuth), an early favorite of longtime fans. Wood is further represented here by "Sin-Doll Ella" (*MAD* #35, September-October 1957), whose conceit is to take the fairy tale of *Cinderella* and treat it as if it were written by Tennessee Williams. As a mounting device, writer Al Meglin (Nick Meglin's brother, and an award-winning dramatic television writer) juxtaposes the film versions of Williams's *A Streetcar Named Desire*, *Cat on a Hot Tin Roof*, and *Baby Doll*. Wood turns in a tour-de-force performance here, expertly capturing the look and feel of these three films and doing wicked caricatures of Marlon Brando, the thumb-sucking Carroll Baker, and Burl Ives as Big Daddy. Mendacity, indeed!

"Backyard Barbeque" (*MAD* #35, September-October 1957) was both written and illustrated by Dave Berg. A charter member of "The Usual Gang of Idiots," Berg would go on to create the long-running and much-beloved "The Lighter Side of . . ." feature.

"*MAD* Bubble Gum Cards" (*MAD* #29, September-October 1956, illustrated by Jack Davis) is *MAD*'s spin on collecting trading cards. At the time, the idea of producing a set of "Famous Cowards" was completely outlandish, but in the many years since there have been any number of trading card sets featuring notorious criminals, murderers, and even terrorists. Another Davis piece appearing here, "*MAD* Builds a More

Civilized Mousetrap" (*MAD* #30, November-December 1956, written by the staff) is considered to be an early *MAD* classic.

Henry Wadswoth Longfellow is given the *MAD* treatment in "The Children's Hour" (*MAD* #32, March-April 1957), charmingly illustrated by longtime *MAD* favorite Don Martin. Another Martin piece (from *MAD* #31, January-February 1957), listed under the heading of "Soft-Sell Advertising Department," was originally part of an ongoing series of Martin "Future TV Ads." Later christened "*MAD*'s *MAD*dest Artist," Martin's early work was much darker and more in the vein of "sick humor" than his later, "sound effect-oriented" style. And concluding the book is Martin's notorious "The Seaside Incident" (*MAD* #35, September-October 1957), which is without a doubt the most darkly sexual strip the artist ever did.

Coming up next from ibooks is a facsimile edition of *The Ides of MAD*, originally published in March 1961. We come to *praise* Neuman, not to bury him!

Grant Geissman *is the author of* Collectibly MAD, *(Kitchen Sink Press, 1995), and co-author with Fred von Bernewitz of* Tales of Terror! The EC Companion *(Gemstone/Fantagraphics, 2000). He compiled and annotated the "best of" volumes* MAD About the Fifties *(Little, Brown, 1997),* MAD About the Sixties *(Little, Brown, 1995),* MAD About the Seventies *(Little, Brown, 1996), and* MAD About the Eighties *(Rutledge Hill Press, 1999). He also compiled and wrote liner notes for* MAD Grooves *(Rhino, 1996), contributed the introduction to* Spy vs. Spy: The Complete Casebook *(Watson-Guptill, 2001), and wrote the introductions to the anniversary editions of* The MAD Reader, MAD Strikes Back!, Inside MAD, Utterly MAD, The Brothers MAD, The Bedside MAD, Son of MAD, *and* The Organization MAD *(ibooks, 2002-2003). When not reading* MAD, *Geissman is a busy Hollywood studio guitarist, television composer, and "contemporary jazz" recording artist, with 11 highly regarded albums released under his own name.*

The other day, we stopped in at our local "art" theater to see a double bill of foreign films ... you know, those imports that are supposed to be free of censorship ... and we made a startling discovery. *They're a fraud!* The first picture was in French, and since we hadn't paid much attention back in High School when we were supposed to be learning the language, we were forced to read the English titles that flashed on the screen. We were following the goings-on pretty well this way, when we happened to notice that the guy with the beret and the pencil-striped moustache on our right was laughing uproariously at parts we didn't think were particularly funny, and snickering knowingly at parts we didn't think were particularly sexy. And the same thing happened to the guy with the handle bar moustache eating the hero sandwich on our left when the Italian picture came on. So it suddenly occurred to us that them English titles don't quite tell *all* that's going on! The way we figure is ..... SOMEBODY'S COVERING UP! Study the following typical scenes we noted, and see if you don't agree that ...

The English titles

the

FOR

MO

don't quite match

action in

EIGN

VIES

THE RESTAURANT SCENE

THE JEWEL ROBBERY

We really should not do this, you know, Jock . . .

I know, Henri. Already my conscience is bothering me!

I know, Henri. I can smell the Gendarmes breathing down my neck!

We will be caught for certain,
you know, Jock . . .

It is only a matter of
time, you know, Jock . . .

I know, Henri. Crime
does not pay!

THE SHIPPING OUT SCENE

Joe! Tell me it isn't true, Joe!

Tell me you're not leaving, Joe!

Not without keeping your promise to me, Joe!

THE STREET SCENE

Hello, Lucille . . .

I've been waiting two hours, Sidney. You're late!

Mother is sick! She's asking for you!

END

LEAD PAN ALLEY DEPT.

We figure, if they keep testing H-bombs, there'll be some changes made over the next few years. Take f'rinstance popular music. Popular music is bound to reflect these changes. So here's our idea of the kind of songs young lovers of future generations will be singing as they walk down moonlit lanes arm in arm in arm in arm ..

the **TOP**

25 Rocks

BOMB SONG HITS

| "A" YOU'RE ABOMINABLE | DON'T STEP ON MY BLUE SUEDE FEET | SAY, SEE BOOM | TILL THE MUSHROOM CLOUDS ROLL BY | I'M WALKING BEHIND ME |

YOU'RE LOATHSOME
TO LOOK AT

JONNIE OSSZEFOGVA

You're lovely to look at,
Delightful to know,
And *forty feet* high.
Because you're up in the sky,
I think the most impossible thing to do
Is walk down a lane holding hands with
       you.
You're lovely to look at,
Delightful to know
But this cannot last.
'Cause when I try to kiss you good-night,
I get nauseous from all that height,
     my dear.

THERE'S NO STREET
WHERE YOU LIVE

SAMMY AXOLOTL
OZGOOD Z'BEARD

I have often walked
    On this street before,
But there once was pavement
    Underneath my feet before.
Now as I walk by,
    I see rubble fly,
Boy, it's *rough* on the street
    Where you live!

People stop and stare,
    They don't bother me!
Got lead underwear,
    I'm safe as safe can be!
All the air is filled
    With radioactivity.
And it's *worse* on the street
    Where you live!

Oh, that frightening feeling
As the glow spreads over the land.
That exposed-to-lightning feeling
When those geiger counters click
    to beat the band!

There are no more trees,
    They've been all knocked down.
You will never hear a bird
    In any part of town.
See the plane draw near!
    Let's get out of here!
Yucca Flats is no street
    Where to live!

Copyright 1976 by Lawrence Welk
Music Corp., bottlers of Vitamin En-
riched Champagne, Bubbles, N.M.

THE THING THAT
I MARRY

WHAT-ME NEUMAN
ALFRED E. WORRY

The girl that I marry
    Will have to be
A purple-skinned beauty
    With two heads or three.

The girl I call my wife
    Will have a nose
With eight nostrils
    You play like a fife.

Her nails will be claw-like,
    And in her hair
She'll wear geiger-counters,
    And I'll be there

'Stead of flyin', I'll be sighin'
    Next to her,
And she'll roar like a lion.
    The girl I propose to
Will have fourteen toes too,
    Like me!

SPACE SHIP

SCHROEDER
"BEE" THOVEN

Space ship,
Space ship,
Go so fast!
Space ship,
Space ship,
Shoot right past!
Earth is no more place to stop!
Since H-Bomb make it pop!

MAMA, LOOK-A H-BOMB

MELVIN COWZNOFSKI

Mama, look-a H-Bomb,
    They shout,
Their mother tell them,
      Watch for fallout!
Look-a your Daddy,
    He know!
Was fallout make him ugly so!

Hit the dirt!
    Join the crowd!
Mama look-a mushroom cloud!
      (repeat)

MY BLUE SHELTER

IRVING POTRZEBIE

Whenever I hear
    A bomb test is near,
I hurry to
    My Blue Shelter.

A hole in the floor,
    A six-inch lead door,
Will lead you to
    My Blue Shelter.

You'll see a smiling face
    Without a trace
Of coming doom.
    A little nest
That's nestled where
    The H-Bombs boom.
Just Molly and me,
    Let's see, that makes three!
We're happy in
    My Blue Shelter.

END

MAD COATS OF ARMS

In the Middle Ages, when you got rich and famous because you could swing a sword faster and better'n the next guy, you got yourself a coat of arms. Every symbol in your coat of arms meant something. Your coat of arms told all about *you* . . . whether you were cowardly or brave, weak or strong, ignorant or stupid. Below the coat of arms was your family motto, usually in Latin so nobody would catch wise. Most coats of arms hung on the walls of old castles, above old fireplaces, next to old broadswords, old paintings and old enemies. Today, hardly anybody who gets rich and famous gets themselves a coat of arms. And today, just because hardly anybody does it swinging a sword is no excuse. So we offer some rich and famous people these coats of arms, free, from Mad.

Liberace

Betty Furness

AUTOMATICA DEFROSTI

Jack Webb

DOM-DA-DOM-DOM

Elvis Presley

IN HOC HOUNDOG

Greta Garbo

I vant to be alone!

Marilyn Monroe

Norman Rockwell

END

26

A SCENE WE'D LIKE TO SEE

The Fighter

2

3

4

"Alice is here, and your mother forgives you!"

11

Interlandi

12

END

SEEING IS BELIEVING

You've heard about this "Picture-Phone"... the coming telephone system where you not only hear, but see the person you're talking to? Well, we at MAD are worried about a big problem its use is sure to create. And we're not talking about the problem: How you gonna answer the "Picture-Phone" when it rings while you're taking a bath? This is no problem for us, since we don't take baths. What we're worried

MAD PICTURE-BACK

FOOL YOUR BOSS...

about is the problem: How you gonna tell them little white lies, when the people you're trying to fool can see for themselves you're a faker? The solution, as we see it, is: Some smart operators . . . Us, for example! . . . should bring out a kit specifically designed for fooling people on "Picture-Phone". You would merely tell them little white lies while standing before old window shades cleverly converted into:

'S
·PHONE
DROPS

39

40

END

FAIR WARNING DEPT.

*And now, MAD, mindful of its responsibility
to readers and anxious to allow them to*

MOTOR

BE

(The cops

< see note>

gain any advantage, however small, over non-readers, presents this next vital article.

IST

WARE !

are on your tail)

First strategic move came when police deduced that isolated two-tone patrol cars were easily recognized by motorists driving all black cars.

Strategic move by police consisted of painting two-tone patrol cars black to match motorists' black cars, thereby forestalling recognition.

WAR OF RECOGNITION

Motorists retaliated quickly by trading in black cars for pastel-colored varieties, thus again isolating rare, out-of-place black patrol cars.

Police Departments around the country are going all-out to enforce the laws of the highways, and rightly so. Yes, even MAD is for highway safety and law enforcement. But it is the method used that we object to . . . method being this trend toward non-police-looking police cars that catch the unsuspecting motorist unawares. Up to now, motorists have been able to cope with the problem of how to recognize police cars (see above), despite the Police Departments' insidious campaign to remain hidden. But recently, MAD learned that the latest move on the part of the motorists (taking to wearing bright hued clothing) has infuriated the Police Departments. After all, an officer of the law must wear a uniform, or else how are people going to respect him? So now, the police have come up with the most devilish

(cont.)

BETWEEN MOTORISTS

Police counterattacked by discarding rare black patrol cars, acquiring new pastel-colored ones to match motorists', again gaining advantage.

plan of all to trap the motorist into the traffic courts. Disguised patrol cars that don't even look like *cars!*

The indignant editors of MAD feel that fire should be met with fire. After exhaustive research we have spied out the majority of disguises planned and are herewith exposing them. We are also preparing a booklet entitled, "How to Disguise Your Car and Thus Avoid Inconvenience."

This booklet will tell how, with a little paint and some minor revisions, you can make your car appear like a small ranch house, a rock garden or a base fiddle. If you wish to obtain this booklet, simply address a card "To whom it may concern" and deposit it in the pouch of any large kangaroo you see at the zoo. We feel that, for the time being, it's best to keep this movement as well-hidden as possible.

AND POLICE TO DATE

Motorists' latest move was to adapt outlandish clothing styles like plaid caps and chartreuse jackets, thus isolating dull police uniforms.

But war of recognition is not yet over. While motorists drive on with a false sense of security, police are readying secret weapons

A WARNING OF THINGS TO COME...NEW SECRET

GOOD HUMOR TRUCK

Police mobile radar unit disguised as a Good Humor truck will check speeding cars. Alert motorists, however, will be able to tell fake police Good Humor truck from real thing. Police Good Humor man will be too busy consulting radar screen to ring his bell. If you see a Good Humor man who is not ringing his bell . . . slow down!

WEAPONS...DISGUISED
POLICE CARS

LEMONADE STAND

Police helicopter disguised as lemonade stand
will hover over highways and trap speeders.
However, alert motorists will be able to tell fake
police stand from real one. Real lemonade stand
will not have rotating umbrella and, depending
on strength of lemonade sold, real stand will
not be more than a foot off the ground. Careful!

FOUR-MAN BOBSLED

BABY CARRIAGE

Innocent-looking baby carriage will be another device to catch erring motorists. Carriage, equipped with 180 horsepower engine, will do 85 mph, accelerating to top speed from a standing start in 12 seconds. Carries one midget policeman inside, regular-sized policeman as steerer. Watch for steerer's retractable roller skates!

Keep an eye out for this baby on hilly highways. Disguised as a four-man bobsled, this device is powered by a 225 hp. engine with a 9.25 to 1 compression ratio and four-speed transmission. It carries two policemen, a recording clerk and a traffic court justice for on-the-spot trials. Watch for tell-tale gavel-rapping anchor man!

SLED AND DOG TEAM

By this winter, police will have put into action patrol unit disguised as Alaskan sled complete with 8 mechanized huskies. A V-1 motor will be concealed in each of the mechanical dogs, giving this job the equivalent of a V-8 dogpower engine. To tell fake police sled and dog team from the real thing on icy roads . . . listen for barking! **END**

NANSY

Recently, while scanning the pages of our favorite newspaper in search of material to swipe, our attention was magnetically drawn to the above comic strip. In fact, every day our attention is magnetically drawn to this comic strip because it always has a simple unique style, because it always has a simple unique gag, and mainly be

by Ernie Brushfiller

cause we've always had a uniquely simple mind. After we read it (and hated ourself for our weakness), we thought about the unique style of this comic strip and how the same strip would look in the unique styles of other comic strips. Here, then, is MAD's version of how those other comic strip's artists would interpret Ernie Brushfiller's . . .

NANSY DUCK

DICK NANSY

LI'L NANSY

NANSY CANYON

END

HOW NOW CHARRED

THESE DAYS, WHEN POP TELLS MOM...

I'm taking you **out** for dinner, dear!

BACKYARD

Barbecues come in assorted sizes and shapes. Simplest of these is the bowl-type, or *brazier*, with a grid top, mounted on tripod legs. This type is perfect for families with very limited backyard space.

COW DEPT.

HE DOESN'T MEAN OUT TO A FANCY RESTAURANT!
HE MEANS HE'S TAKING HER **OUTSIDE**, TO THE . . .

BARBECUE

Then there is the portable type of barbecue, mounted on wheels. This type affords convenience and mobility to the barbecue chef, and also comes in handy for chasing and pinning any guest who seems reluctant.

And then there's the super-type of barbecue, which is actually a converted blast-furnace. This explains why most outdoor chefs turn out hamburgers that are heavy as lead.

STARTING FIRE

The inexperienced chef lights his barbecue fire the hard way. First, he laboriously covers his charcoal with bits

The connoisseur of backyard barbecues lights his fire the easy way. First, he douses his charcoal with a specially.

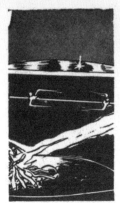

of paper and twigs, and then he touches his match to it. ▶
The fire fizzles out before charcoal-broiling can begin.

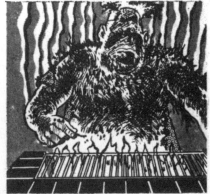

made inflammable fluid, and then touches his match to it.
The charcoal-broiled-meat aroma can be smelled for miles.

TESTING WIND DIRECTION

Always test the wind direction before you start the fire.
Smoke may blow into house, forcing you to move barbecue.

Disadvantage of brick barbecue is now obvious. Smoke may
blow into neighbor's house, forcing you to move family.

MAKING SHESHKABOB

This popular barbecue recipe is made by alternately impaling choice pieces of meat and vegetables on a long spit,

then revolving slowly over the coals. This is what is known as "done to a turn". The true outdoor chef, however,

uses genuine cavalry sword instead of spit. That way, if anybody refuses to eat the mess, he can run him through.

TOSSING SALAD

Place lettuce, tomatoes, raw carrots, cucumbers and salad oil in neat pile.

For that extra kick, add a pineapple.

Barbecue salad will be nicely tossed.

BROILING STEAK

Steaks should be broiled to individual
tastes. Some people like them rare . . .

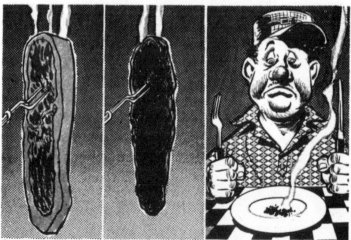

Some people like Some people like But most people will get
them medium rare. them well-done. them burned to a crisp!

FUTURE OUTDOOR LIVING

Backyard barbecues have become so popular, architects who design our future homes are planning to eliminate kitchens altogether. In fact, the more extreme elements among them

are predicting a return to the primitive cave-like dwelling. They figure, if people are going to insist upon *eating* like cave men, then they might as well *live* like them.

END

AND SO, ONE PREPOSTEROUS ARTICLE
FOLLOWS ANOTHER. EVER DEDICATED TO
THE CAUSE OF WIDENING AND IMPROV-
ING ITS SCOPE OF READERS' INTERESTS,

MAD BUBBLE

You know how all those bubble-gum cards you ever collected up to now have been nothing but portraits of famous national figures, past and present, like for instance
famous baseball heroes or famous war heroes or famous
western heroes. You know how after a while you get sick
and tired of famous heroes. Day after day, gum-wad after

SMEDLEY Van STURDLEY

"Nobody's home!"

MAD NOW OFFERS HOBBYISTS AMONG YOU A RARE OPPORTUNITY. BE THE FIRST IN YOUR NEIGHBORHOOD TO BEGIN THIS EXCITING AND UNUSUAL COLLECTION OF ...

GUM CARDS

gum-wad, the same old famous heroes. Well, dear readers, here's your chance to get out of the rut. Here's your chance to throw away that dull old collection of corny bubble-gum cards featuring world famous heroes. Here's your chance to begin a dull *new* collection ... with this MAD starter-set of corny bubble-gum cards featuring world famous clods.

MAD GUM

1

SMEDLEY Van STURDLEY

Oaf
Concord, Mass.

Born: December 5, 1748
Height: 4'—3"
Weight: 109

When Paul Revere made his famous ride from Lexington to Concord, arousing the colonists at every Middlesex village and farm and warning them that the British were coming, it was Smedley Van Sturdley who **turned over and went back to sleep!**

FAMOUS COWARDS No. 1

©M.B.G.

Printed in U.S.A.

MILTON FORBISHER

"I lost my head!"

MAD GUM 2

MILTON FORBISHER

Minute Man
Boston, Mass.

Born: October 9, 1752
Height: 7'—7"
Weight: 109

At the battle of Bunker Hill, when that handful of Minute Men made their valient stand against an overwhelming force of red-coated British regulars, it was Milton Forbisher who panicked and shot before he saw the whites of their eyes!

FAMOUS COWARDS No. 2

©M.B.G.

Printed in U.S.A.

STANLEY HENKLEDORF

"I'm gettin' out a' here!"

MAD GUM 3

STANLEY HENKLEDORF

Poltroon
Getzville, N. Y.

Born: July 3, 1788
Height: 5'—8"
Weight: 109

During the war of 1812, at the famous naval battle of Lake Erie, when Commodore Perry, in the thick of the fight uttered those immortal words, it was Stanley Henkledorf who heedlessly turned, took to a long boat, and **did give up the ship!**

FAMOUS COWARDS No. 3

©M.B.G.

Printed in U.S.A.

WALTER N. GOOBER

"I forget!"

MAD GUM 4

WALTER N. GOOBER

Malingerer
Pecan Gap, Tex.

Born: August 7, 1808
Height: 6'
Weight: 109

In the war of independence between Texas and Mexico, after General Santa Anna and four thousand Mexicans besieged and massacred Colonel William B. Travis and his gallant band of one hundred and eighty men, it was Walter N. Goober who **refused to remember the Alamo!**

FAMOUS COWARDS   No. 4

©M.B.G.

Printed in U.S.A.

BEAUREGARD BORDON

"Mooooooo-Hah!"

MAD GUM 5

BEAUREGARD BORDON

Born: September 14, 1859
Weight: 1090

Bovine
Manassas Va.

In the first pitched battle of the Civil War, General Johnston's Confederate forces opened fire on General McDowell's Union forces at Sudley's farm in Manassas, Virginia. Beauregard Bordon was caught in the middle, hence the name of this battle . . . boy, you should have seen that **bull run!**

FAMOUS COWARDS   No. 5

Printed in I.N.K.

Just so people won't get the idea that MAD is a magazine strictly for clods, we've decided to get a little arty . . . and illustrate a famous poem. Here, then, for all you arty clods, is Don Martin's interpretation of . . .

THE
CHILDREN'S HOUR

By Henry Wadsworth Longfellow

Between the dark and the daylight,
When the night is beginning to lower,
Comes a pause in the day's occupations,
That is known as the Children's Hour.

I hear in the chamber above me
The patter of little feet,
The sound of a door that is opened,
And voices soft and sweet.

From my study I see in the lamplight,
Descending the broad hall stair,
Grave Alice, and laughing Allegra,
And Edith with golden hair.

4

A whisper, and then a silence:
 Yet I know by their merry eyes
They are plotting and planning together
 To take me by surprise.

5

A sudden rush from the stairway,
 A sudden raid from the hall!
By three doors left unguarded
 They enter my castle wall!

6

They climb up into my turret
    O'er the arms and back of my chair;
If I try to escape, they surround me;
    They seem to be everywhere.

7

They almost devour me with kisses,
    Their arms about me entwine,
Till I think of the Bishop of Bingen
    In his Mouse-Tower on the Rhine!

Do you think, O blue-eyed banditti,
  Because you have scaled the wall,
Such an old mustache as I am
  Is not a match for you all!

I have you fast in my fortress,
  And will not let you depart,
But put you down into the dungeon
  In the round-tower of my heart

And there will I keep you forever,
Yes, forever and a day,
Till the walls shall crumble to ruin,
And moulder in dust away!

END

DATING DEPT.

Since you are obviously a failure in the dating department, (You wouldn't be wasting time reading this trash if you could be going

THE

DATING

Up to now, you have probably approached the problem of dealing with the fair sex in one of two ways. You've either been the "shy" type, and you've failed miserably, or you've been the "aggressive" type, and you've failed miserably. Now, MAD shows you how to be the "Mad" type, and

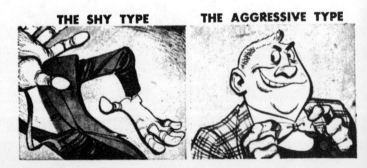

THE SHY TYPE   THE AGGRESSIVE TYPE

out with girls!) MAD now offers you a rare opportunity to overcome your difficulties with this article which explains . . .

MAD

TECHNIQUE

fail miserably. All kidding aside though, let's go through a typical date, and see how these three types would handle the very same situations. When you've finished, it will be obvious to you that you've made many bad mistakes in your time, including starting this article in the first place.

THE MAD TYPE

ASKING FOR THE DATE

THE SHY TYPE hasn't enough nerve to ask for date, writes note instead, pays kid to deliver it. Unfortunately, girl usually accepts, goes out with the kid.

THE AGRESSIVE TYPE has plenty of nerve, asks girl for date right out. Unfortunately the girl also has plenty of nerve and she usually refuses outright.

THE MAD TYPE doesn't bother to ask, shows up at the girl's house with flowers, asks if she's ready. She hasn't enough nerve to admit she forgot date.

SECURING TRANSPORTATION

THE SHY TYPE hasn't the nerve to ask for his old man's car, so he rents one.

THE AGGRESSIVE TYPE doesn't even ask for his old man's car, he just steals it.

THE MAD TYPE not only borrows old
man's car, he also borrows the old man.

IMPRESSING THE GIRL'S FATHER

CHALLENGED BY DATE'S FATHER to Indian wrestle, the shy type purposely loses match, impresses father as a clod.

CHALLENGED BY DATE'S FATHER to Indian wrestle, the aggressive type throws father, impresses him as a clod.

CHALLENGED BY DATE'S FATHER to Indian wrestle, the MAD type throws mother, impresses father as great guy.

IMPRESSING THE GIRL FINANCIALLY

THE SHY TYPE impresses his date by inadvertently leaving a big tip. He's too chicken to ask the waiter for change.

THE AGGRESSIVE TYPE impresses his date by impulsively leaving big tip. He eats candy-bar lunches all that week.

THE MAD TYPE impresses his date by
deliberately leaving a big tip. He cleverly swipes it all back as he leaves table.

LOOKING FOR A LITTLE PRIVACY

THE SHY TYPE stops car, pulls old routine about being out of gas. Date gets mad, so he ends up walking down dark lonely road to distant service station.

THE AGGRESSIVE TYPE stops car, pulls 'out-of-gas' routine. Date gets mad, he gets mad, so she ends up walking down lonely dark road to a distant bus stop.

THE MAD TYPE doesn't resort to any corny routines. He crashes the car into a tree, and they *both* end up walking down that dark lonely road. Hoo-hah!

END

93

ANOTHER SCENE WE'D LIKE TO SEE

Escaping the Cannibals

END

Continuing its campaign of examining and extolling man's progress in his many fields of endeavor, MAD now turns its attention to the world of science, specifically to the complex art of modern photography, and in this next factual article (watch what happens when you turn the page) analyzes reasons

WHY

the precision engineered, highly perfected...

35 mm Camera

STACK OF RARE COINS
VIEW FINDER
FINDER FINDER
SHIRT BUTTON
CAMERA BUG
LENS BUTTON
EXHAUST
GENUINE LEATHER
ON SWITCH
OFF SWITCH
LENS SHADE
ROULETTE WHEEL

ESCAPE HATCH
WINDER
SIDE WINDER
REWIND WINDER
RANGE-FINDER WINDER
RANGE-FINDER FINDER
RANGE (ELECTRIC)
LIGHT METER
CHANNEL SELECTOR
ELECTRIC METER
METER METER
DRAIN PLUG

REPLACED

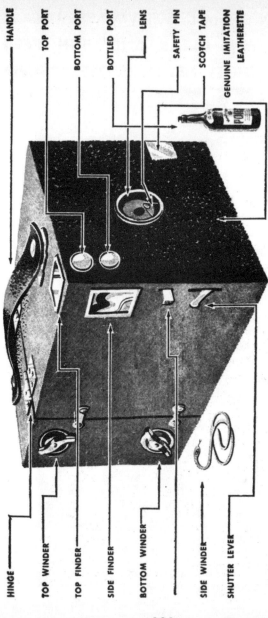

the simple, unpretentious, primitive

Box Camera

HANDLE

TOP PORT

BOTTOM PORT

BOTTLED PORT

LENS

SAFETY PIN

SCOTCH TAPE

GENUINE IMITATION
LEATHERETTE

HINGE

TOP WINDER

TOP FINDER

SIDE FINDER

BOTTOM WINDER

SIDE WINDER

SHUTTER LEVER

101

MODERN 35mm CAMERA MAKES IT EASY TO GET FINE DETAIL AND HIGH-SPEED ACTION SHOTS NEVER BEFORE POSSIBLE

USING OUTMODED box camera, MAD's Seymour Fudd took this picture of a farmer and his children seated in a pasture. Note stiff, posed attitudes of subjects, lack of action, and blurred head of bull grazing contentedly in background. Nervous bull moved slightly while picture was being taken.

USING MODERN 35 mm camera, MAD's Wally Balloo caught this exciting shot of the same farmer and his children. Note how movement is stopped, showing subjects in midst of wild scramble. Nervous bull, grazing in background, suddenly charged wildly, enraged by Balloo's popping flashbulbs.

WITH OLD-FASHIONED BOX-CAMERA, AS PHOTOS BELOW BY *MAD* LENSMEN FUDD AND BALLOO CLEARLY DEMONSTRATE

ABOVE PICTURE, taken by photographer Fudd, is another example of failing of undeveloped box camera. Due to fixed-focus lens, close-up shots are impossible, and all Fudd could get were dull shots like this one of a Bikini-clad model.

HOWEVER, with perfected 35 mm camera, plus portrait attachment, photographer Balloo was able to move in, capture amazing close-up-detail shots just like startling picture above of the same Bikini-clad model.—Interesting, huh?

Now let's compare quality of the box

Study actual-size contact print (above) made
from film shot with old-fashioned box camera.
Note that images in picture are strangely fuzzy,
gray, and lacking in definition. Now compare to
actual-size contact print (right), made from film
shot with modern 35mm camera. Note that images
in picture are sharp, clear, well-contrasted, and
mainly impossible to see with the naked eye.
However, this one drawback can be quickly reme-
died. With the use of expensive equipment, en-
largement (upper right) can be produced, equal
in size to box camera print, with images that are
strangely fuzzy, gray, and lacking in definition.

camera picture with 35mm camera picture!

Wally Balloo, MAD photographer, with equipment used in conjunction with 35mm Camera

(a) Ever-ready camera case. (b) Tripod. (c) Flash gun.
(d) Flash bulbs. (e) Exposure meter. (f) Lens cap.
(g) Filters.   (h) Filter adapters.   (i) Strobe light
(j) Power pack for strobe light.   (k) Enlarger.

TOTAL COST: $1326.45

IN THIS ARTICLE WE HAVE EXAMINED AND EVALUATED REASONS THE 35mm CAMERA

Seymour Fudd, MAD photographer, with equipment used in conjunction with
Box Camera

(a) Film.   (b) Sun.

TOTAL COST: 45¢

REPLACED THE BOX CAMERA. NOW FOR US, JUST ONE QUESTION REMAINS UNAN-SWERED: *WHY?*

E N D

ONCE UPON A TIME DEPT.

These days, fairy tales are big business. Take the story of Cinderella, the little girl with the weird taste in shoes. First, Walt Disney made millions on his animated version. Next, Leslie Caron danced her psychiatric way to a box-office bonanza. Then Rogers and Hammerstein guaranteed their old age security·with a TV spectacular composed of leftover

SIN-DOLL

Tennessee

ACT I, SCENE 1: Curtain rises on disgustin' decayin' bedroom of disgustin' decayin' shack in disgustin' decayin' South. Heroine, Ella, sleeps in southern comfort with a

tunes from South Pacific. And recently, the Saddler's Wells Company cashed in on their ballet interpretation. So who are we to fight a trend? Here, then, in an effort to make a quick buck, is our brand new version of that over-worked fairy tale, Cinderella, written especially for MAD by a world-famous, ultra-sophisticated Broadway playwright . . .

ELLA
by
Williamsburg

bottle (or is it with a bottle of Southern Comfort?). MUSIC: A few disgustin' decayin' bars of Eli Whitney's "Get Yore Cotton' Pickin' Hands Off Mah Gin". . .

ACT I, SCENE II: Light gradually to give effect of summer evening. There's an aroma of magnolias, the hum of insects, the singin' of birds, an' the sounds of a barnyard chorus, all emergin' from orchestra pit.

SPECIAL EFFECT: Fairy Godmother appears in a puff of smoke. If stringent state censorship prevails, clothes can easily be substituted for puff of smoke.

114

117

ACT II: The Ball. Colored lights fill room as Southern damsels blush behind fans. Nearby, Confederate soldiers converse profanely. That's why Southern damsels blush

behind fans. Big Fat Daddy eyes damsels. His son, Prince Kowalski, eyes Confederate Soldiers. Ella enters ball-room, followed by Fairy Godmother . . .

Ah shore hopes tonight's assortment of delectable damsels will inspire yo into takin' a wife, m'boy. Ah see that gal who jus' entered has caught yo eye. Is yo starin' at her lovely face, or her lovely figger?

122

125

129

Time for the commercial, gang...so here we go with another sample Story Board of...

FUTURE
TV. ADS

2

3

5

Whaddya gonna do? Sleep all day? Gonna lose your new job like ya' did the last eight? Honestly, George, what's wrong with you lately? George?

133

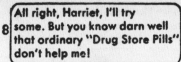

Wow, Harriet! I feel great! What did you say was the name of those pills I just took?

14

15

SCIENCE DEPT.

When Milwaukee's Donald Knuth first presented his revolu-lutionary system of weights and measures to the members of the *Wisconsin Academy of Science, Arts, and Letters*, they were astounded...mainly because Donald also has two heads. All kidding aside, Donald's system won first prize as the "most original presentation". So far, the system has been adopted in Tierra del Fuego, Afghanistan, and Southern Rhodesia. The U.N. is considering it for world adoption.

THE POTRZEBIE SYSTEM
OF WEIGHTS
AND MEASURES

This new system of measuring, which is destined to become the measuring system of the future, has de-cided improvements over the other systems now in use. It is based upon measurements taken 6-9-12 at the Physics Lab. of Milwaukee Lutheran High School, in Milwaukee, Wis., when the thickness of MAD Magazine #26 was determined to be 2.26334851-7438173216473 mm. This length is the basis for the entire system, and is called one potrzebie of length.

The Potrzebie has also been standardized at 3515.-3502 wave lengths of the red line in the spectrum of cadmium. A partial table of the Potrzebie System, the measuring system of the future, is given.

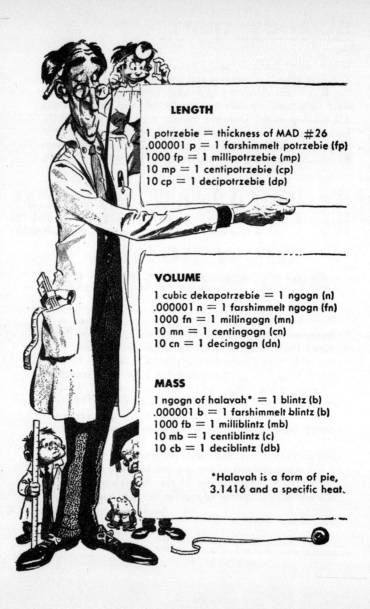

LENGTH

1 potrzebie = thickness of MAD #26
.000001 p = 1 farshimmelt potrzebie (fp)
1000 fp = 1 millipotrzebie (mp)
10 mp = 1 centipotrzebie (cp)
10 cp = 1 decipotrzebie (dp)

VOLUME

1 cubic dekapotrzebie = 1 ngogn (n)
.000001 n = 1 farshimmelt ngogn (fn)
1000 fn = 1 millingogn (mn)
10 mn = 1 centingogn (cn)
10 cn = 1 decingogn (dn)

MASS

1 ngogn of halavah* = 1 blintz (b)
.000001 b = 1 farshimmelt blintz (b)
1000 fb = 1 milliblintz (mb)
10 mb = 1 centiblintz (c)
10 cb = 1 deciblintz (db)

*Halavah is a form of pie,
3.1416 and a specific heat.

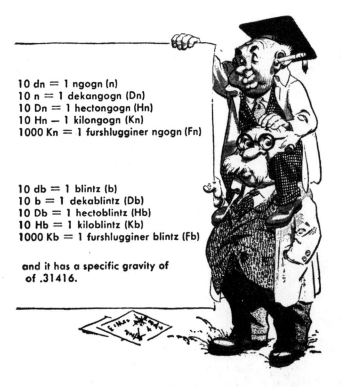

10 dp = 1 potrzebie (p)
10 p = 1 dekapotrzebie (Dp)
10 Dp = 1 hectopotrzebie (Hp)
10 Hp = 1 kilopotrzebie (Kp)
1000 Kp = 1 furshlugginer potrzebie (Fp)

10 dn = 1 ngogn (n)
10 n = 1 dekangogn (Dn)
10 Dn = 1 hectongogn (Hn)
10 Hn — 1 kilongogn (Kn)
1000 Kn = 1 furshlugginer ngogn (Fn)

10 db = 1 blintz (b)
10 b = 1 dekablintz (Db)
10 Db = 1 hectoblintz (Hb)
10 Hb = 1 kiloblintz (Kb)
1000 Kb = 1 furshlugginer blintz (Fb)

and it has a specific gravity of
of .31416.

TIME

1 average rotation of the earth = 1 clarke (cl)

.00001 cl = 1 wolverton (wl)

1000 wl = 1 kovac (kv)

100 kov = 1 martin (mn)

100 mn = 1 wood (wd)

10 wd = 1 clarke (cl)

10 cl = 1 mingo (mi)

10 mi = 1 cowznofski (cow)

DATE

October 1, 1952 is the day MAD was first published according to the old calendar. On new calendar, this is price 1 of cowznofski 1. Cowznofskis before this date are referred to as "Before MAD (B.M.)" and cowznofskis following this date are referred to as "Cowznofsko Madi (C.M.)" The calendar for each cowznofski contains 10 mingos named as follows: 1. Tales (Tal.) 2. Calculated (Cal.) 3. To (To) 4. Drive (Dri.) 5. You (You) 6. Humor (Hum.) 7. In (In) 8. A (A) 9. Jugular (Jug.) 10. Vein (Vei.)

142

FORCE (absolute)

a force which, when acting upon 1 blintz of mass for 1 kovac, causes it to attain a velocity of 1 potrzebie per kovac = 1 blintzal (b-al).
1000000 b-al = 1 furshlugginer blintzal (Fb-ál)

ENERGY AND WORK

1 blintzal-potrzebie = 1 hoo (h)
1000000 h = 1 hah (hh)

POWER

1 hah per kovac = 1 whatmeworry (WMW)
1000 WMW = 1 kilowhatmeworry (KWMW).
100 KWMW = 1 aeolipower (A.P.)

RADIOACTIVITY

The quantity of radon which is in equilibrium with one blintz of radium = 1 hyme (how's your mom, ed)

HEAT ENERGY

The amount of heat necessary to raise one blintz of hala-vah 1° S = 1 vreeble (v.) 1000 v = 1 large vreeble (V)

TEMPERATURE

100° Smurdley (S) = optimum temperature
for eating halavah (27°C.)

COUNTING

48 things = 1 MAD
49 things = 1 baker's MAD

ANGULAR MEASURE

100 quircits (''') = 1 zorch ('')
100 zorch ('') = 1 zygo (§)
100 zygo (§) = 1 circle or circumference

BASIC CONVERSION

1 inch = 11.222 potrzebie
1 mile = .71105 Fur-potrzebie
1 blintz = 36.42538631 grams
1 kiloblintz = 80.3048 pounds
1 Fur-blintz = 36.425 metric tons
1 ngogn = 11.59455 cc = .0125 qts.
      = 2.3523 teaspoons

MISCELLANEOUS MEASUREMENTS

1 light Cowz. $= 1.14 \times 10^{12}$ Fp.

1 vreeble $= 574.8$ hah

1 cosmo per sq. potrzebie $= 3.1416$ bumbles.

1 faraday $= 122300$ blobs/blintz equivalent weight.

1 electron-ech $= 5.5794 \times 10^{15}$ hoo

1 blintz molecular wt. of a gas $= 77.4$ Cn

Density of $H_2O = .31823$ blintzes per ngogn (distilled water).

1 atmosphere pressure $= 1.4532 \dfrac{b^2}{p}$

335.79 p of Hg.

1 b $= 3234.4$ b-al

gravity $= 3234.4$ p per kov. per kov.

speed of light $= 114440$ Fp/Kov.

FACTORS (ABBREVIATED TABLE)

1 potrzebie $=$ 2.2633 millimeters
.089106 inches

1 Furshlugginer potrzebie $=$
2.2633 Klm.
1.4064 miles

1 centimeter $= 4.4182$ potrzebie

1 kilometer $= .44182$ Fur-potrzebie

1 wood $= 144$ minutes

1 kovac $= .864$ seconds

1 year $= 3.6524$ Cowznofskis

1 watt $= 3.499651$ Whatmeworries

1 Horse Power $= 2.57$ Kilowhatmeworry

1 Aeolipower $= 38.797$ Horse Power.

1 vreeble $= 34.330$ calories

END

DEAD

Since we don't make enough money to live on when we write this trash, we recently took a night job spinning cobwebs in the "Dead Letter" section of New York's Main Post Office. Seeing all those undelivered letters caused us to speculate . . . might not the world be a lot different today if they had reached the people for whom they were intended? So we opened a random few to prove our point. Another point we prove is—you can get arrested tampering with U. S. Mail!

LETTERS

John T. Stuart
Attorney-At-Law
Springfield, Illinois

April 3rd, 1865

A. Lincoln
The White House
Wushington, D.C.

Dear Abe:-

Saw "Our American Cousin"
when it played Chicago.
It's a bomb! Do yourself
a favor. Stay home!

John

Sept. 24, 1948

Miss Marylin Monroe
% Schwabs Drug Store
Hollywood and Vine
Hollywood, California

Dear Miss Monroe:-

Your application to join the Salvation
Army has been approved by this office.
Kindly report to our School for Officers
Training in San Francisco, on October 9th,
1948, at 10 A.M.

Bless you,

Emilia Dermquod

Emilia Dermquod
Brigadier

THE MILLS HOTEL
Transient and Resident Accommodations for Single Men.

May 19, 1927

Charles A. Lindbergh
Roosevelt Field
Mineola, L. I.

Mon cher Charles,
    Am unavoidably delayed.
Will not make scheduled
take-off time. Wait for me!

    You cannot find Paris
without me.

        Your co-pilot,
        Gaspard ,

July 22, 1886

Miss Tillie Monohan
242 Flatbush Avenue
Brooklyn, N.Y.

Dearest Tillie,
My heart is ~~bor~~ broke
because you have refused
my proposal of marriage.
I will be on the Brooklyn
Bridge tomorrow at 4 P.M.
Meet me there and tell
me you have changed your
mind.
Otherwise I will kill
myself!!
No kiddin!
Steve Brodie

150

COOK COUNTY BOARD of HEALTH
Chicago, Illinois

October 1, 1871

Mrs. Gertrude O'Leary
Cor. Jefferson & DeKoven Sts.
Chicago, Illinois

Dear Mrs. O'Leary:-

It has been brought to our attention by
complaints from your neighbors, that
you are harboring a live cow in a resi-
dential area of Chicago proper, contrary
to Provision 189, Section 4, Cook County
Health Code.

Please be advised that if you do not re-
move said cow from your area by October
8, 1871, you will be subject to a fine
in the amount of $2.00.

Respectfully yours,

Melvin J. Finnigan

Melvin J. Finnigan
Commissioner of Health

Cuartel General de la Marina
REAL ARSENAL NAVAL
LA HABANA, CUBA

January 20, 1896

TO: Captain Charles D. Sigsbee, USN, Commanding
U.S.S. Battleship MAINE
Naval Station
Key West, Florida, U.S.A.

FROM: Capitán de Navío Edelmiro Gonzales
Commandant of Port Facilities,
Havana, Cuba.

Dear Captain Sigsbee:-

It is with pleasure that we learn of your impending good-will visit to our fair city on the magnificent American Battleship MAINE. Please be advised that our Corps of Engineers will be carrying on blasting operations for the purpose of deepening Havana harbor, so may I respectfully suggest that when you arrive, you anchor safely outside of the harbor limits.

Cordially yours,

Edelmiro Gonzales

Capitán de Navío
Royal Spanish Navy

U. S. MALE DEPT.

These days, men aren't "men" unless they read "men's" magazines. And "men's" magazines aren't for "men" unless they're full of "he-men" type articles. So MAD wouldn't be "mad" if it didn't poke some fun at "men's" magazines like:

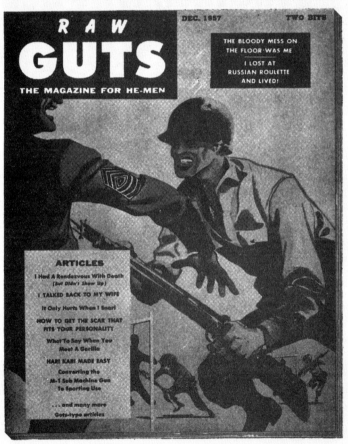

t The AMAZON!

by Mickey Cohen

MVMBA, our guide, staggered into camp with the news. Up ahead, a giant Armadillo was pinching female members of the Itchigoochi. The Itchigoochi were friendly. We couldn't let them down! Only the river stood between us. The mighty Amazon River. We had to cross it. But how? It was too late to rent a canoe. There was only one answer.

Sturdley was the first to hit the water. One after the other, we all followed suit, hitting the water. It was a most grotesque spectacle. Imagine! Grown-up men hitting and punching innocent water! CONTINUED

Illustrations by Matt Tisse?

155

Illustrations by
Rem Brandt

I
CAPTURED
SIX JAPS
WITH ONE
HAND!

by Lt. Col. William "Willie" Sutton

It was the most terrifying experience of my life. Just think of it. Six one-handed Japs. How they were ever taken into the Japanese Army, I'll never know. And I didn't wait to find out. When they came marching toward me, each with his one hand raised in surrender, I took off for H. Q. They had quite a job keeping up with me, as

CONTINUED

Illustrations by Leo Nardo

I Fought A
GRIZZLY BEAR
BLINDFOLDED!

by Al Anastasia

How a big old grizzly like that ever managed to get himself blindfolded is beyond me. But he sure looked funny as he charged. I couldn't help but laugh in his face as his huge paws closed around me in a crushing embrace, he looked that funny.

Even now, as I look back on it, lying here in the hospital room, I have to laugh. Only I can't because it hurts

CONTINUED

I Warned The Warden
That I Would
BREAK OUT!

by Johnny Dio

The fool didn't believe me. So I showed him, the next day. It was the worst break-out he'd ever seen at Leavenworth. My whole body was covered with these big, ugly purple blotches. The doctor had warned me about my allergy to Lasagna and Chicken Fat. And there it was on my mess tray, the very first meal.

CONTINUED

158

Illustrations by
Sal Vadordali

I FOUGHT

With The Boys Of The

26 th INFANTRY

by Maj. Gen. Frank Costello

Yes! I fought with the boys of the 26th Infantry! I also fought with the boys of the 39th Infantry! Then I fought with the boys of the 47th Infantry! It seems that I just couldn't get along with anybody while I was in the army.

I remember as a child that I used to fight with all the kids on my block

CONTINUED

I CLEANED UP AN
ENEMY OUTPOST
BARE-HANDED!

by Sgt. John Dillinger D.O.A.

Lucky for me, there was nobody there at the time. Nevertheless, it was a risky proposition . . . cleaning it up barehanded. They didn't even give me a decent broom.

One thing I can say about being a P. W., the German policy on treatment

CONTINUED

Illustrations by P. Casse

160

HE WAS AN OLD LION KILLER!

by Lucky Luciano

The only trouble was, there just weren't any more old lions around to kill. And the young ones were much too ferocious for him.

He had to find some other way to release his deep-rooted hostilities.

And so, that's how Fenwick Furd started molesting young innocent

CONTINUED

Illustrations by Della Croix

THERE'S MANY A SLIP

Science, in its never-ending march of progress, dedicated to improving man's lot on Earth (or blowing the place up in the attempt!), has somehow neglected one of the most important functions of life. Eating! When it comes to the dining room table, we're still in the Middle Ages. Those

MAD

UTEN

knives, forks, and spoons we use today to spill stuff **on** our best ties are basically the same as the ones the Romans used to spill stuff on their best togas. Nobody ever bothered to redesign them and bring them up to date. Nobody, that is, until now. Now, *we* try . . . and fail . . . with

EATING

SILS

While careful grafting and cross-pollinating has eliminated most of the seeds from the popular grapefruit, no one has been able, as yet, to eliminate its squirt. Scenes like one at left can be eliminated once and for all with MAD's

**SQUIRTPROOF
SELF-WIPING
GRAPEFRUIT SPOON**

Before the beer foams up and cascades down the sides of the glass all over your hand, one thing to do is blow it off, as fellow in scene at left is doing. But if you're sick of the bartender punching you in the eye, use MAD's

**FOAM-CATCHING
BEER GLASS**

If you've ever struggled with spaghetti, you know what torture fellow on left is going through. No matter how much you wind and wind, you still end up with strands of the stuff dangling down your chin. So stop buying new ties. Use MAD's

NO-HANG SPAGHETTI FORK

There's nothing quite as frustrating as that last drop of delicious soup or fruit-cup juice you just can't scoop up unless you break every rule of etiquette and tilt the dish. Now you can suck it all up with the straw built into MAD's

LAST DROP SOUP AND FRUIT CUP SPOON

Here's another familiar problem: how do you keep those elusive little devils, carrots and peas, from rolling off your fork and sloshing gravy on your brand new sport shirt like guy on left is doing? The answer is simple: just use MAD's

CARROTS AND PEAS SPEARER

If you are like Susan, the lazy housewife on the left, you are sick and tired of that pile of dinner dishes every night. And who can blame you? But have you ever asked yourself if dishes are really necessary when you can use MAD's

LAZY-SUSAN DISH-SAVER

If you're a mixed-drink man, and you've had it as far as choking on all those ice cubes you accidentally swallow, or as far as watered-down highballs are concerned, then you'll hail MAD's

**NO-DILUTING
ANTI-CHOKE
DRINK GLASS**

Invariably, when you're invited out to someone's house for dinner, they serve steak. And invariably it's tough. When you try cutting it with an ordinary knife, what happens is pictured at left. Beat this problem by bringing your MAD

**TOUGH MEAT
BUZZ-SAW KNIFE**

If you're a tea drinker, or you switched recently because you like Arthur Godfrey (there are such people!), then you know how, when you wring out the teabag so it won't drip on the tablecloth, it drips on the fingers. Well, not with MAD's

TEA BAG
SQUEEZER

Take a nice fresh slice of white bread, and try buttering it with cold hard butter. You know what happens. The same thing that's happening to the guy on the left. Total destruction. But it won't happen if you use MAD's self-heated

COLD BUTTER
SPREADER

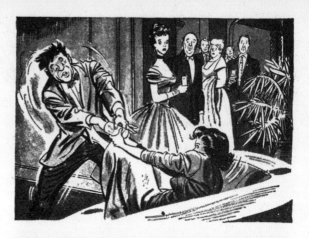

A baffling problem that plagues the Martini set is: how to fish out the olive, cherry, or onion once the drink's gone. Spearing it with fingernail is frowned on. The only solution is MAD's

COMBINATION COCKTAIL-STIRRER CHERRY-NETTER

Slob on left has just finished cool glass of milk. Note tell-tale white moustache on top lip. If this happens to you, you too are a slob. Remain a slob and still enjoy cool glass of milk without that tell-tale moustache. Use a MAD

NO-MOUSTACHE MILK GLASS

Ever try to butter hot corn-on-the-cob? Ever try to hold it and eat it after you finally do get it buttered? If you have, then you'll surely appreciate the new MAD

**SELF-BUTTERING
NO-TOUCH
CORN-ON-THE-COB
HOLDER**

Biggest problem facing the American people is: how does one watch TV and eat dinner at same time without having to look down to see what to scoop up next, thereby missing what happens on screen? Answer: shovel food direct from MAD's

**NO-LOOK-DOWN
TV TRAY**
END

END

Leave us face it . . .

. . . this is a heck of a

Uncivilized, isn't it? And yet, in the homes they share all over the country, millions of innocent American mice are daily meeting this same sudden cruel fate. Think about this for a moment or two. Think hard about this. Think of *yourself* in this mouse's shoes. By George, you'll *have* to think hard about this, since any fool knows mice don't wear shoes!

MAD BUILDS A
MOUSE

thing to do to a mouse!

All kidding aside, this article has been written because MAD has a conscience. This article has been written because MAD has a feeling for poor little animals. But mainly, this article has been written because MAD has these eight pages to fill up. And so, on these eight pages, MAD suggests six new approaches to the problem of trapping mice. On these eight pages . . .

MORE CIVILIZED
TRAP

Culture-loving mouse passes through attractive entrance (A) of trap designed to look like high class art gallery (B). Corridors (C) and (D) are lined with framed microscopic reproductions of valuable old masters. Door to salon (E) has sign (F) announcing special showing of original world famous painting of the Mona Lisa. Excited mouse rushes into salon (G), sees frame (H) with canvas (I) slashed to ribbons (J), and has heart attack.

Muscle-flexing, he-man-type mouse is urged by cleverly-worded sign (A) to prove strength by slamming lever (B) with sledge-hammer (C) sending weight (D) up wire (E) ringing bell on top (F). Gullible mouse confidently makes attempt (G) but ingeniously tapered wire (E) prevents weight (D) from reaching bell (F). Stubborn mouse, after trying in vain all night, collapses from exhaustion.

Science-Fiction-minded mouse, lured from hole (A) by strange recorded sound (B), watches in awe as mechanical flying saucer (C) makes simulated landing. Mouse's excitement mounts as door in saucer (D) opens and ladder (E) is extended. At sight of emerging horrible alien creature (F), terrified mouse drops dead.

Civic-minded mouse sees marquee (A) announcing big mass-meeting political rally, eagerly enters doorway (B) of trap designed to look like huge auditorium jammed with stuffed mice (C), moves down aisle (D), slides into only available seat (E), turns attention to rabble-rousing mechanical speaker (F) delivering tape-recorded political address (G), and is scalded to death by blasts of hot air.

Reader-of-Mad-Type Mouse, attracted from hole (A) by current issue of this magazine (B) opened to this article (C), sees sheer idiocy of suggested civilized approaches (D, E, F, G, & H), knows that old-fashioned gadget is only effective method of trapping mice, and dies laughing.

Neurotic-type mouse impulsively enters door (A) of trap designed to look like mouse-psychiatrist's office (B), lies down on couch (C), tells all to mechanical nodding mouse-analyst (D) for usual hour session (E), is then handed bill (F), and at sight of outlandish charge (G), blows top.

END

185

The Railroad Timetable

At first glance a railroad timetable appears to be cluttered, unreadable and senseless. Actually, it is! Study this timetable of one of America's least-traveled lines, the Chicago, Lasagna & South Gasp Railroad. After you've finished, we here at MAD are certain you'll conclude the only way to travel is by car...

CHICAGO, LASAGNA & SOUTH GASP RAILROAD

ALL CATTLE CARS ARE AIR-CONDITIONED

For equipment needed to survive on these trains see p. 8

Miles	WESTBOUND (*Read down—How else?*)	Elev.		21 Daily	7 Ex. Sun. D	11 Ex. Sat.	23 Daily	101 Weekly	5739 Monthly	65 Hardly
				AM	AM	AM	AM	AM	PM	PM
	Train			THE AARDVAK xx Will not run Dec. 25, Jan. 1 or any other day, for that matter.		THE CALVIN COOLIDGE f Will not run, even if nominated.	T THE SILK STOCKING n If caught, will run.	THE ANARCHIST tt No baggage, no passengers, no engineer.		THE MUDDER ss Will not run if track is fast.
0	CHICAGO	351	Lv.	1 06	2 14	6 11	6 12	6 13	3 56	5 31
10	Ulcer	1577	Ar.		2 59	7 30	......		7 15	......
215	E. Frammis	2344	"		5 16	9 14pp	......		......	......
215½	Frammis	4432	"		5 09	10 02	......		......	10 30
215	W. Frammis	2443	"		5 17	7 15	8 20z		......	......
230	Neumanville	4567	"		10 45				......	......
235	Fort Fungus, Iowa	5678	"		3 11		9 14		......	......
240	Slump City	6	"		4 35				......	......
245	Gopher Prairie	17	"		5 55				......	......
260	Haggenfranz	2	"		5 56				......	......
281	Undertow	–37	"		8 09				......	......
300	Elbowgrease	–688	"		10 55			6 14	......	......
319	Whoops, Missouri	1	"	3 11	1 03			......	......	......
324	K-k-k-kankakee	?	"	3.46jj	1 31q			......	......	......
325	W. Crocus, Iowa	5	"	8 02	5 43			......	......	......
326	Lake Pheugfth	10	"	11 51	7 00		......	......	......	......
327	LASAGNA	15	"	1 05	7 17	12 35	8 30	6 15a	......	......
370	Buzzardville	20	"	10 14	11 30	......	1 54	......	......	12 15vv
381	E. Asterisk, Arkansas	25	"	......	1 05H	......	......	......	......	......
394	Munch	30	"	......	2 34hh	......	......	......	......	......
402	Crunch	No!	"	4 19	2 34ll	......	4 45kk	......	......	......
411	Hopeless Crossing	101	"	......	9 30K	......	......	6 16AA	......	......
901	Snerdsberg, Tennessee	6¼	"	5 03rr	9 56	......	......	......	......	......
912	Toadstool	5¾	"	......	9 59	......	......	......	......	4 45c
934	Ft. Apache, Arizona	4001	"	......	*1 34	*4 45	*2 36v	......	......	......
937	Bedspring j	88	"	......m	1 56p	......	......	......	......	......
944	Buckskin	888	"	......	......	......	......	......	......	......
952	Riboflavin sss	8888	"	4 15	......	......	......	......	......	......
963	New Molar, California	3481	"	6 17y	......	......	......	......	......	......
981	Fritter o	31	"	9 55	......	......	......	......	......	8 30
999	SOUTH GASP	0	"	10 30	10 30	10 30	10 30	10 30		10 30

EXPLANATION OF REFERENCE MARKS

- a Does not stop on odd-numbered Thursdays.
- AA Adjust oxygen masks.
- c When the engineer feels like it.
- D Not this Sunday.
- f Does not carry passengers born in the month of May.
- H Train whistle hits a perfect high "C" at this point.
- hh Stops to let off paying passengers.
- ll Stops to throw off non-paying passengers.
- j Station Master noted for repertoire of snappy stories.
- jj Rarely on time.
- K Stops to throw Mama from the train a knish.
- kk Last week.
- m Tomorrow.
- sss Sun rises at 7:00 a.m.
- n Observation car carries spittoon once used by William Jennings Bryan.
- o Nice looking blonde sells candy here.
- pp Look, Ma! No hands!
- p Avalanche!
- q See note "a."
- rr Last call for dinner.
- ss Conductor's middle name is Sidney.
- T All seats on this train reserved in advance, otherwise you got to sit on your luggage.
- tt Friendly pickpockets in club car.
- vv Four-day layover.
- v Alternate Mondays.
- xx Don't order corned beef and cabbage in the diner unless you have supply of Bicarbonate of Soda along.
- y Bus leaves every hour for Jamaica, Post time: 3:45, Pari-Mutuals at the track.
- z If you're lucky.
- * Mountain time prevails in this territory, but trains are operated under Central Time. For equivalent Pacific Time, figure one hour earlier than Mountaim Time and two hours earlier than Central Time if you got the time.

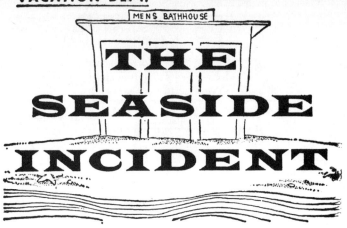

THE SEASIDE INCIDENT

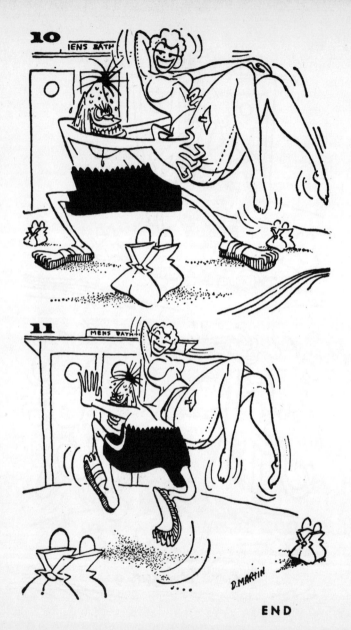

END

ALSO AVAILABLE!

INSIDE MAD
0-7434-4480-9

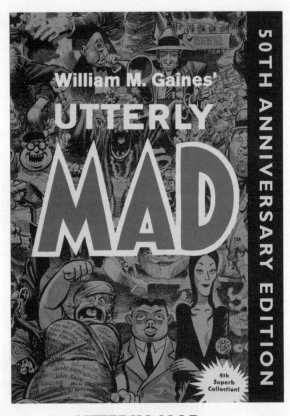

UTTERLY MAD
0-7434-4481-7

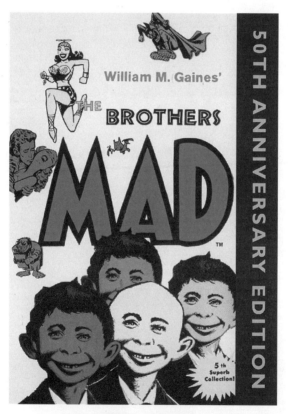

THE BROTHERS MAD
0-7434-4482-5

THE BEDSIDE MAD
0-7434-5910-5

SON OF MAD
0-7434-7496-1

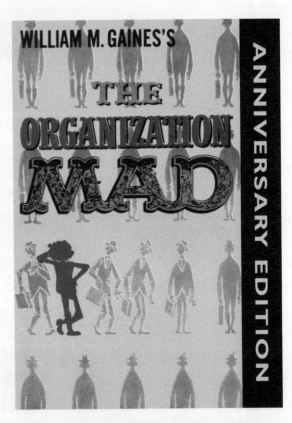

THE ORGANIZATION MAD
0-7434-7477-5